# Ready

## Ready to Speak Out

# Ready

Ready to Speak Out

By

T & I

Tonita Walker & NNylari Iralynn

T & I

# Copyright 2024 by Tonita Walker and NNylari Iralynn

All rights reserved.

ISBN: 9798336846959

Published in the United States by

Tonita Walker and NNylari Iralynn

Newnan, GA 30263

www.tandimusic.com

Ready

**This book is dedicated to every person who has been traumatized by your past and have a desire for change. Know that there is a very present help in the Lord.**

**T & I**

Ready

# Chapter one

## Avery's Random Hook Up

**T & I**

# Avery's Random Hook Up

Spotlights fill the center of the stage, lighting up a dark room with music playing loudly in the background as Avery takes the stage. Skin glowing, and a face mask over her face to protect her identity, Avery puts both hands on the pole and begins to swing her body around and around, legs up, legs down, twisting, bending, turning, and entertaining the men as dollars hit the floor right below her. Pole dancing was Avery's secret life but, Avery was a famous singer who traveled the world on tour. While she was a man's fantasy, in her mind she was reliving being another man's prey as a child but at least this time she got paid for it. It's late and the customers have begun to leave the building. Avery makes her way backstage to shower and change her clothes so that she can head home. She begins to have flash backs to a time when she had no control over who, what, when and where someone could touch her.

Tears begin to run down her face as she walked past the other girls in the room on her way to the shower. Avery stops at her makeup station and grabs a bottle of champaign and continues to walk towards the bathroom.

## Ready

When she reached the bathroom, she shuts the door behind her and slowly falls to her knees sobbing as a rush of bad memories hit her like a tsunami. It was as if she was there again but watching herself from outside of her own body. The older version of herself was fighting back but her younger self didn't have the strength to do a thing. Avery can see her younger self being forced down a dark hallway into a room on the left at the end of the hall. She was told to open the door and go in. Avery turns the knob of the door, pushes the door open, and walks in, and as soon as she walks in someone quickly closes the door behind her and that's when Avery realizes that she isn't alone in the room. One of her older male cousins is in the room with her. Avery turns around and runs back to the door and tries to open it but someone on the other side is holding the door shut.

Avery grabs the bottle of wine, takes the top off, and turns the bottle all the way up, drinking half the bottle before putting the bottle back down. Before she knew it, thirty minutes had past, and she was wasted. Struggling to get her balance, and falling a few times, Avery finally gets off the floor and manages to get undressed and gets into the shower.

## T & I

Avery staggers her way to her car after a long night of partying and entertaining strange men for money. No shoes on and barely any clothes on, she manages to get her car door open and get into the driver seat but soon after, she's fast asleep at the wheel and she sleeps through the whole night in her car with unlocked doors and purse nowhere to be found.

Avery awakes to a beautiful sunset hitting the front glass of her car. As she struggles to open her eyes, she feels the weight of last night's events quickly hit her. Her head is pounding, makeup messed up and her mind all over the place, she begins to cry sorrowfully because she knows she messed up again. Avery thinks to herself, "why do I keep doing this to myself. I don't want to keep living like this, I hate it." Just as she puts her key in the ignition the owner of the club knocks on her window. Avery looks over to find him holding her purse and shoes and shaking his head at her. Avery opens the car door and grabs her things from him, says thank you, and shuts the door. As she puts on her seatbelt and looks up into the mirror, she catches a reflection of herself and she's see how

## Ready

messed up she is but because she doesn't know how to fix herself, she shakes it off, puts her car in reverse, backs up and then drives away.

Avery arrives home safely and decides to wash her face then she gets to work on her music for her next set. She begins to write about how much pain she feels on the inside and how much she wishes she were dead. Avery starts thinking about her sister Ava and just when she decides to pick up the phone to call her, Avery's manager Gavin calls to remind her of the next show she has to sing at, and for her to have her bags ready for the car to pick her up. Avery is a little upset because she thought she had at least a day away from performing but instead of complaining, Avery grabs a bottle of wine and a champagne glass. Drinking and sex with random men is her poison and her way of escape these days but she can remember a time when her relationship with her sister helped her through the dark times.

## T & I

Avery was raped and molested so much as a child that now she is numb to sex. In her mind she has separated her emotions from the act but not realizing that it all affects her negatively.

It's 6 a.m. the next day and Avery is passed out on the floor from doing her normal routine. Avery's ride will be there in a few hours. The random guy she slept with last night is awake and getting dressed in the room. He comes out and tries to wake Avery up because he remembers Avery saying something about a ride coming to pick her up at 8 a.m. He picks Avery up and takes her to the bathroom, sits her down on the toilet, turns on the faucet to get some cold water and he splashes some on Avery's face to wake her up. Avery's eyes open quickly. Looking confused and somewhat embarrassed, she pauses and then says, "who are you and how did you get in my house?" The guy replies, "I'm the pizza guy from last night. You jumped on me last night and pretty much took my clothes off for me and well…… you know the rest." Avery shacks her head and starts crying. "I am so sorry, please forgive me for doing that, I was drunk, but thank you for taking care of me." The guy replies, "no

## Ready

problem, I had a great time. I'll leave my number by the bed. The guy walks out of the bathroom, finds a pen and paper, and leaves his number by Avery's bed and finds his way out of Avery's house. Avery jumps in the shower and prepares herself for the day.

By the time Avery's ride arrives, she has put herself together, popped a few pills, and drunk two cups of coffee. Completely wired, Avery makes her way to the car with a few travel bags in hand. The driver gets out to open Avery's door for her and reaches out to take the travel bags from her and Avery says, "hi, thank you. The driver responses and says, "your welcome madam." Avery gets in the car and releases a huge exhale as the driver shuts her door. Keep it together, keep it together, Avery whispers to herself. The driver puts Avery's bags in the trunk, gets in the driver seat and takes off. Avery puts on some dark shades, so she isn't recognized why she's out. The driver tries to make small talk with Avery, but Avery is fast asleep with her head propped up against the door frame.

## T & I

The car comes to a stop and Avery's still asleep in the back seat. The driver gets out and comes around to her door and opens it and Avery falls out of the car in shock. The driver says, "I'm sorry madam I didn't realize you were asleep on the door." As the driver helps Avery to her feet, Avery says, "it's okay, it was totally my fault." Avery stands to her feet, and she realizes that the driver was still holding her hand and Avery was somewhat drawn to him, so she invites him in the establishment to help her with her bags. They enter in the back of the building where all the performers arrive, and Avery goes straight to her private dressing room. When she reaches the door, she looks around to see if anyone was there. When she saw that she and the driver were alone, she invited him into her dressing room. "Come on in and you can just put my bags down by the makeup counter," she said. The driver responded, "yes madam." While the driver was putting Avery's bags down for her, Avery was making sure her dressing room door was locked. Avery quickly walks up to the driver and when the driver stood up from putting her bags down Avery jumped on him, hugging him tightly and began to kiss him on the lips. The driver pulls back from her and says, "wait, wait, I'm a married man." Avery

## Ready

response and says, "she doesn't have to know." The driver gives in, and Avery continues to kiss him on lips and before you know it, the driver pushes Avery towards the makeup counter, pulling her dress up quickly as Avery unbuttons his pants. This was the moment Avery did something she said she would never do, sleep with a married man. In the moment Avery had no remorse and no thought to who or how it would affect anyone else, she just wanted what she wanted. They both climax and someone knocks on the door. Avery quickly pulls her dress down and the driver fixes his pants and swiftly walks to the door, opens it, and says, "excuse me" as he walks past Avery's manager Mr. Gavin. Gavin looks the driver up and down as he walks past and shacks his head as he enters Avery's dressing room. "Avery…. There you are... How's my girl?" Avery responses and says, "hey Gavin, in a good mood today I see." Hahahahaha… "I could say the same for you" Gavin replied. Avery says, "what's that supposed to mean." Gavin reaches in to hug Avery and says, "nothing, nothing at all, you know I love you sweetheart. I just want you to be careful." Avery hugs Gavin back and rolls her eyes but doesn't give him a response. Gavin assures Avery that she wouldn't be at this event

## T & I

long and that she can leave right after she performs and then he leaves her dressing room. Sitting in the makeup chair, Avery looks up at herself in the big mirror on the walk and she begins to cry. Someone knocks on Avery's dressing room door. Avery whips her face quickly and says, "it's open, come in." It's her makeup artist Melanie. Melanie has been her close friend since high school. When Avery realizes who it is at the door she stands up and then runs to her arms and just breaks down in tears. Melanie embarrasses Avery with loving arms and tells her it's going to be okay.

**Ready**

# Chapter Two

### Avery's Dream

**Ready**

# Avery's Dream

After drinking and dancing the night away Avery falls asleep on the floor wherever she lands and begins to dream about her childhood. Vivid memories resurface of when she had secret friends in her bed as her sister Ava lay asleep just a few steps away. Avery and Ava's mother's name was Joyce, and she had a voice that was angelic. Joyce was an amazing mother and wife. She spent most of her time with her kids but the one night she decides to take a chance and trust a family member was the worst decision she would ever make. Starring at the small light near her bed on the nightstand, Avery feels the warmth of her mother helping her say her prayers and softly singing her a bedtime song. Joyce gently placed her right hand on Avery's head pushing back her curly Afro textured hair, she leans down to kiss Avery's forehead, then she whispers, "I love you" sweetly in Avery's ear, seats back up on the bed and smiles and says, "good night baby." Avery smiles back at her mom and watches as her mom gets up from the bed and do the same to her younger sister and then walk to the door to leave. Pulling the door closed slowly, Avery's mom is in a happy place with no thought of the danger that was lurking around

## T & I

her children. Avery turns over to her left side in her bed with her face facing the wall. Hours go by as Avery and her sister Ava sleep deeply. Avery's mom gets a call in the middle of the night. It's her uncle Elroy calling to tell her that her mother was rushed to the hospital, and she needs to get there as soon as possible. Uncle Elroy tells Avery and Ava's mom that he's right around the corner and he can come watch kids until she returns from the hospital. There mom agrees to let Uncle Elroy babysit until she returns from the hospital. Uncle Elroy knocked on the front door and Avery's mom lets him inside, tells him where all the emergency information is and then she quickly gets dressed, runs out to her car and heads to the hospital.

The kids have no idea that her mom has left the house or that anything has happened as the kids are still sleeping. Meanwhile, Uncle Elroy stood in the barely lit living room and began to pace the floor nervously trying to talk himself out of what he really wants to do because he knows it's wrong, but he can't seem to shake the appetite for little girls. Uncle Elroy's urge was more powerful than his will power to do the right thing,

**Ready**

so he gives in to the urge and takes advantage of this unfortunate situation. He was going to do the unthinkable to another innocent young girl.

Uncle Elroy has made up his mind, he was going to get what he wanted. Uncle Elroy takes off his shoes and leaves them next to the sofa in the living room so that he can quietly slip into the girls bedroom. He walks over to the bedroom door; he places his right hand on the doorknob and turns the knob slowly trying not to wake anyone. When the knob is fully turned, he opens the door slowly and walks in shutting the door behind him. Uncle Elroy walks slowly over to the side of Avery's bed and begins to take off his clothes and drop them on the floor. He looks at Avery laying there in the bed and is immediately aroused. Moving slowly, he pulls back the covers from the bed and off Avery's tiny little body. Uncle Elroy gets in the bed with Avery, spooning her from the back, he places his hand on her waist and begins to slide Avery's little nightgown up until he reaches her panties. Ava wakes up and begins to turn over to face Avery's bed when she hears movement in their room. Ava looks over to Avery's bed to find Uncle Elroy in the bed with her, but she remains quiet out of total confusion of what is going. Uncle Elroy gently pulls Avery's underwear down to her ankles trying not to wake her, but Avery wakes up, turns around and before she could scream Uncle Elroy places his big hand over Avery's mouth as Avery wiggles and tries to kick. Uncle Elroy puts his leg over Avery's legs, places his other arm over Avery's body to keep her still and he whispers in her right ear, "shut up, shut up, if you scream or tell anybody I will kill your little sister right now, your mom, and your whole family." Avery stops screaming and trying to fight as Uncle Elroy takes his leg off her, rubs his hand against Avery's little arm, then he pulls Avery's nightgown all the way up to her flat chest and places his hand on her tiny belly and slowly works his hand down to her private area and begins to tough her and get her ready to penetrate. Ava wants to scream for help for her sister but she's afraid of what Uncle Elroy might do, so she lays quietly in her bed crying for her sister as Uncle Elroy takes what he wants. He rubs her tiny private area over and over until he thinks she is ready for intercourse. He takes his hand and spits on it and then rubs it on his private area and proceeds to lift up Avery's leg and shoves himself inside of her. Avery is in tears

## Ready

uncontrollably as Uncle Elroy strokes her over, and over again causing Avery to bleed out on her bed. This was the moment Avery died on the inside. Uncle Elroy climaxes inside of her and then jumps up off the bed. Avery lay still in the bed in a state of shock as Uncle Elroy says, "clean this up and don't tell or I will kill you and your family." Ava is still laying in her bed crying in shock. Avery sits up slowly on the bed, dries her tears, pulls off her underwear from around her ankle, slowly moves her legs to the side of the bed and painfully stands up. The pain she felt was unthinkable. As she begins to pull the bloody sheets off the bed, she feels some liquid running down her legs. She looks down to see what it is and its blood and some foreign liquid she's never seen. Avery gathers the bloody sheets, walks over to Ava's bed and tells her, "stay quiet, its going to be okay." Then she quickly makes her way down the hall to the laundry room and manages to put her bed sheets in the washer. Afraid that someone might find out. She pours bleach and detergent into the washer, turns on the washer and then walks to the bathroom and shuts the door behind her. Uncle Elroy steps outside to smoke a cigarette to calm his nerves. Avery turns on the shower, pulls off her clothes and gets in the shower. Dropping to the floor of the shower, Avery begins to cry. Her hair gets soaking wet as the water falls on her head. She stays in the shower for hours scrubbing her body trying to get his scent off her. She scrubs and scrubs, but in her mind, it seems to do nothing. It was embedded in her mind now. Avery was traumatized. Life as she knew it was no more. Avery turns off the water, grabs a towel and steps out of the shower she notices that she's still bleeding so she grabs a lot of tissue and puts it in her underwear, and gets dressed. She opens the bathroom door to find Uncle Elroy seating on the sofa waiting for her to come out of the bathroom and he stops her by saying, "are you alright?" Avery replies, "yes" and proceeds to walk back to her room. Uncle Elroy yells out, "I put some new sheets on your bed." Avery shuts her bedroom door and locks it. She looks over at Ava in her bed and she is fast asleep. So many thoughts and scenarios race through Averys mind at that moment. She wondered where her mother was, she wondered why her mother didn't just take them with her wherever she went, she wondered why this had to happen to her, she wondered if she would ever stop bleeding, she wondered if the tissue she placed on her private area would keep the

## Ready

blood from coming through her underwear and she wondered what she would do if Uncle Elroy decided to come back in her room. Not wanting to make a sound, Avery gets in her bed and cries herself to sleep. Nothing would ever be the same.

Avery wakes up from her dream realizing that her dream was actually her memories and all of it was true. She lived it. Avery cried because she remembered how helpless she was and how much she wished things were different.

# Chapter Three

**She played house with me**

**Ready**

# She played house with me

It's another night at the club pole dancing and Avery's not feeling well. She finds herself drunk and high in the locker room after hours again. Unable to make her way out to her car, Avery falls asleep in the lounge chair half naked. Drifting off into a dream about her past as a kid again. Avery remembers having such a sweet grandmother and grandfather growing up. Grandfather was always out working somewhere so she didn't get to spend as much time with him as she wanted to but Avery love him so dearly. Her grandmothers was very open, giving, caring, and kind to them when they came to visit. Avery's grandmother was such an amazing cook and she had a beautiful smile. She was a beautiful person inside and out. Every time Avery asked her grandmother for something she wanted her grandmother would always tell her she could have it even when she should have told her no. She was the glue of the family and everyone in the family respected and loved her.

 It's a beautiful summer day and the wind hits Avery's face as she rode in the back seat of the car with her mom and sister. They were on their way

## T & I

to grandma's house to stay for the day while their mom went to work. Asia the car pulled up to the grandma's house Avery and Ava begin to get excited because they can see their cousins in the front yard playing and they are anxious to play with them. The car stops and everyone gets out. Avery and Ava run straight to their cousins playing in the yard and join in on the fun. Meanwhile their moms goes in the house to let their grandma know that they have arrived and she would be back to pick up the girls after work. Their mom comes back out of the house and says, okay girls I'll see y'all after work, be good okay. Avery and Ava yell back "yes ma'am" and then continue to play.

The house is filled with her grandkids big and small. Most of the little kids are outside playing various games while the older teenagers were inside hanging with each other listening to music. Playing outside, making up games, watching television, listening to music or just talking were the main options of things to do growing up. Hours go by and their grandma has decided to leave the house to run a few errands. Running a few errands for grandma was more like a whole day out on the town. It seemed like she would be gone all day. Grandma comes out of her room

## Ready

walking slowly, calling for the older teens sitting in the to the living room to watch the younger kids while she's goes to the store for a little while. The older teens reply "yes maam" as she leaves out of the front door. As their grandmother gets inside her car, shuts the door and drives off Sheila, one of the older teenagers looks out the window to watch her grandmother leave. Sheila watches the her grandmothers car go down the long drive way and up the hill until she can no longer see her car. She waits a few more minutes before she acts on her plan. Avery is outside in the front yard playing with her cousins when Sheila opens the window to the front bedroom of their grandparent's house to yell out to Avery to come in the house. Sheila says, "Avery, come in the house for a minute." Avery turns to look at where the voice is coming from and then says okay I'm coming. Avery takes her time walking to the house. She makes it the house and walks up the steps, opens the front door and walks right past her other older teenage cousins sitting on the couch in the living room still listening to music. Avery walks down the hallway and opens the first door on the right and walks in. Sheila is still in the window looking out with her arms propped up on the window when she hears Avery open the

## T & I

door. Sheila closes the window and then tells Avery to shut the room door and lock it behind her. Not thinking anything of what Sheila just said to her, Avery closed the door and locks it. Sheila says, do you want to play house with me. Avery replies yes with a big smile. Sheila tells Avery to come sit in her lap, so Avery walks over to Sheila and sits in her lap and Sheila tells Avery that she's going to be the baby and she will be her momma. Avery says okay and then Sheila lays Avery back in her lap and tells her to do what momma tells you to do. Avery says okay. Sheila opens her legs and then positions Avery little tiny behind in between her legs and she begins to make moments rocking from side to side and opening her legs and closing them as Avery tiny back side rubbed in between Sheila's private area. Sheila then took on of her hands and lifted up her shirt, pulled out her breast and put her nipple inside Avery's mouth and began to say "suck that big titty, suck that titty" repeatedly as she continued to move her legs open and shut as Avery back side rubbed Sheila's private area. Avery was in shock as her little eyes moved from each corner of the room and then back up to the ceiling. Avery was confused. She didn't feel safe but she continued to play along until her

## Ready

cousin Sheila made a loud noise that Avery had never heard before and then it all stopped. Sheila took her breast out of Avery's mouth and pushed her off of her lap and told Avery to go back outside and play. Avery did what Sheila said but she was so confused as to what had happened in that room that day. Avery never told a sole.

Its 5 a.m. and Avery is awakened by the cleaning lady vacuuming the rugs in the room at the club. Avery sits up slowly and tears began to fall down her face as she remembers what she dreamed about that night. She was like a scared innocent little girl in a grown woman's body crying out for her mom. She just couldn't make sense of what had happened to her. Her childhood was taken by force and she was left with a painful scream on the inside that no one could seem to hear. Nobody was there to wipe her tears. She played house with her little body and violently stripped away Avery's voice and all of her innocence as she fulfilled her sinful, lustful passion.

# Chapter Four

### Avery's Final Moment

# Ready

## Avery's Final Moment

Its 11:45p.m. and Avery just had another epic performance. The crowd is still going wild as she exits stage right with a very hot outfit on, made of pleather, high heels on her feet to match, and smokey eyeshadow on as if she were into Goth. She walks directly to her manager Gavin and Gavin hands Avery a purple towel to dry off the sweat from her face. "Job well done sweetheart," Gavin says to Avery and Avery says, "thank you" as they both walk back to Avery's dressing room. Gavin opens the dressing room door for Avery and Avery walks into the room. Avery walks straight to the counter where all the mirrors are and begins to just stare at herself. Then one of her assistances walks over to her and begins to unzip the back of Avery's performance clothing and Avery puts her head down and just begins to soak in everything that had happened during her day. She thinks of how she is living out one of her dreams but part of her is unhappy. Avery is given a robe to put on, jeans and a t-shirt to slip on for the ride to the hotel. Avery puts on the robe and then proceeds to walk to the restroom and shuts the door behind her. She sits down on the toilet and stays there for a good 5 minutes. Five minutes feels like an eternity to Avery because her mind continues to wonder back to her childhood and causes her to have a panic attack. She tries to keep herself together but it's too late. She finds it hard to breath and her thoughts rush in like a tsunami. The touching, the tears, and the blood overtake her in the moment, and she breaks down and ends up falling off the toilet and on to the floor on to her knees, holding her arms together as if she were trying to make herself feel safe but it just doesn't work. The floor is full of her tears as she cries out loudly to God asking Him to make it all go away. The more she allows her mind to drift back there the harder it is for her to breath. "God please, please, please just take it away. I don't want to hurt anymore, I don't want to feel anymore, I don't want this burden anymore." Her manager starts to knock on the door, "Avery, who are you talking to in there? Are you okay? We're on a schedule, you have 10 minutes to get dressed and come out and take pictures and sign some autographs for your fans. Avery quickly wipes her face and shakes it off and replies, "Be out in a few minutes." Gavin says, "Okay," as he walks away from the bathroom door to sit down on the couch to wait on Avery to come out.

## Ready

Avery exits the restroom fully dressed and ready for pictures, interviews and signing her autograph. Gavin and Avery leave out of the dressing room and walk to the lobby to greet Avery's fans. Security guards pop out of nowhere and begin to protect Avery from the people in line waiting as Avery walks past them all to get to the table where she will sign autographs. Avery sits down at the table and the rodeo begins. Avery spends hours taking pictures, fake smiling, and laughing with her fans and signing autographs. Two hours have passed, and Avery has met her last fan and now she's ready to leave and head to her hotel for the night. Gavin gets Avery to her car and tells her driver to take her straight to her hotel room and make sure she enters alone. The driver says, "I will get her there safely." Avery arrives to the hotel safely and after making sure Avery gets to her hotel room, the driver leave.

Avery waits an hour before she leaves her hotel room to go downstairs to the hotel bar to get drunk. While sitting at the bar, Avery sees a tall dark chocolate man on the other side of the bar. He looks up and they lock eyes. He then gets up and walks over to Avery. You here alone he ask? Not anymore says Avery. Have a seat Love. What are you drinking

## T & I

beautiful? She looks at him seductively and replies, I'm drinking scotch on the rocks, but I can handle whatever you're buying baby! Avery and her newfound friend drink their way back to her hotel room and just as Avery opens the hotel room door, Mr. Dark chocolate says, well beautiful it was nice meeting you and turns to walk away. Avery grabs his hand and pulls him inside the room and says the night doesn't have to end here baby! Avery and Mr. Dark Chocolate begins to kiss as they make their way to the bed. As they passionately kiss, they begin to pull each other's clothes off. Rough sex, soft sex, it was all a part of the menu that night. They both climax and quickly fall asleep. The next morning Gavin calls. Avery awakes to the phone ringing and rolls over in the hotel bed to find that Mr. Chocolate wasn't just a good dream. Mr. Chocolate was a real thing that happened in her bed last night. She thinks to herself, "It happened again! I don't even know his name!" She picks up the phone. Good morning, Gavin. You did it again didn't you Avery, Gavin says. Avery replies, "what, no. See you're always underestimating me. I don't do that anymore." Avery hears a knock on her door, and she tells Gavin to hold on as she gets up to walk to the door and opens it. Its Gavin

# Ready

standing at the door holding his phone to his ear. Avery is so surprised to see Gavin that she has no words and Gavin says, "surprise surprise Avery" as he makes his way past Avery. Gavin, I wasn't expecting you here so early, Avery says. Gavin walks right to Avery's bed and says, "I see you forgot about the man that's still in your bed. When is this going to stop?!" Let me explain, Avery says. In a disappointed voice Gavin's says, no need, just get him out of here now. Avery walks over to Mr. Chocolates side of the bed and shakes him and tells him that its time to leave. Mr. Chocolate gets up, puts on his clothes, and shoes and walks towards the door. He stops just before he exits the room and says, are you going to call me? Avery replies, get out please. Mr. Chocolate opens the door and walks out. Avery takes her walk of shame to the table where her manager is sitting and takes a sit. She begins by saying, I'm sorry Gavin, I know I said this wouldn't happen again, but I realized that I really have a serious problem and I think I need help. Gavin replies, I'm glad you've finally admitted that this problem is real. Now we can get to work on getting you together and making your life better. I think the first step is to get you into counseling. Are you on board? Yes, I'm ready, I can't keep doing this to myself, and I don't want to live like this anymore. I know I deserve something better.

Gavin gets on the phone with his assistant Melanie and instructs her to schedule Avery an appointment with a good counselor today if possible. Gavin hangs up the phone and tells Avery to take a shower and get dressed for the appointment he is hoping to have for her later that day. Avery does what Gavin asked. An hour has passed. Melanie calls Gavin back with an appointment for Avery at 2p.m. the same day. Avery shows up on time for her appointment with Dr Hicks. She fills out all the necessary documents and Dr. Hicks calls her into her office to begin their first session. Hello Avery, my name is Dr. Hicks. It's a pleasure meeting you and I am looking forward to this new journey we're about to embark on together. So, tell me, what brings you to my office today?

Avery begins to speak. Well…. I guess the best place to start would be the beginning. So here goes… When I was a little girl, I had such a great childhood until that one night when my innocence was taken from me, and it then seemed to just keep happening. My mind is on rewind or instant replay of what happened. I'm covered in blood and its running

## Ready

down my legs and there's this unknown liquid mixed in the blood that I had never seen as a child. I know what it was now, but it traumatized me still to this day. My Uncle Elroy took what he wanted from me, my cousin, she took what she wanted from me, and they never paid for how much they hurt me because I was too afraid to tell anyone. I can still feel his rough hands toughing me like I was a prize he had won. Why did my mom have to leave us with him? Why did he have to touch me? It's just not far. As Avery broke down the details of what happened throughout her childhood, Dr Hicks took notes and allowed Avery to have her moment. Over the next four months Avery continued to meet with Dr. Hicks to talk out her problems and Dr. Hicks interacted with her and gave Avery homework, self-work, and tasks to do to help Avery begin to change some areas in her life and start healing from her childhood traumas. Avery was becoming a whole new person as she worked towards forgiving her uncle, herself, and cousin. But there was another issue that Avery had to get out of her system. Avery and her sister Ava had a falling out years ago and they just never reconnected.

## T & I

Avery's been in counseling for almost six months, and she has reached some amazing milestones during her treatment. Dr. Hicks suggested that Avery go to alcohol anonymous (AA), but Avery didn't believe she had a drinking problem and to prove that, Avery started reducing her alcohol intake and now she has a better relationship with drinking and is able to handle drinking responsibly and her random sex partner fun has completely stopped. Avery seems to be making better choices and creating a new chapter in her life's story.

Avery just arrived back in town from being on a two weeklong tour and now it's time for another session with Dr. Hicks on this beautiful Wednesday morning. Dr. Hicks has asked Avery many times before about her relationship with her sibling, but Avery always declines to speak about her but today Dr. Hicks is hopeful that Avery is in a better place to talk about her sister after months of counseling sessions. Avery arrives at Dr. Hick's office bright and early and she's in a good mood. The receptionist calls Avery's name and lets her know she can go right in to see Dr. Hicks. Dr. Hicks is sitting in her chair right beside the couch where she normally sits. Avery walks into the office and says, "hi Dr,

# Ready

Hicks." Dr. Hicks replies, well hello Avery, I'm so glad to see you. You seem to be in a good mood today. Avery replies, "I am, it's been a good morning and God has really been good too. I never thought I could get to this place but I'm grateful..." I'm so glad to hear that Avery and that lets me know that you're ready to go deeper, so let's get started, says Dr. Hicks. Avery says, "let's do it doc." Dr. Hicks starts out congratulating Avery on accomplishing her goal of getting her drinking under control, getting her sex life under control, fighting through her fears and being honest with herself about where she was emotionally and doing the work to fix it. "Avery I would like to open a new chapter in our sessions and allow you to tell me about your relationship with your sister Ava, says Dr. Hicks." Avery's eyes get really big as she takes a deep breath and then exhales slowly. Avery replies, oh wow Dr. Hicks, you just really know how to throw punches and wake a sister up ha ha ha….. okay let's go there, its time….. okay let's see…. First let me start off by saying that I now have a relationship with God. A friend of mind invited me to come to church a few months ago and I've been going ever Sunday since. I realized that God was the main missing piece in my life, and I can do nothing without Him, so I am finally able to face the darkness of my past and walk down forgiveness street. Ava is my little sister and at one point in our lives were the best of friends. We had an amazing childhood together until we started experiencing traumatic experiences. It made us closer in a survival kind of way and because we truly loved each other as sisters. We were always there for each other, we had sung together, played barbies together, burned our dolly's hair together, shared secrets, and my mom even made us matching outfits. We made a promise to each other that we would always sing together so we formed a group and one day we were approached by a big-time record label called Tony Records. They said we had the whole package but there were also some back-office conversations going between our music producer and Tony Records. You gotta be careful who you have on your team because you never know what their motives are. Our music producer at the time was only after the money and keeping it coming. My sister and I didn't know what our producer was up to but one day I got a call to come meet with our music producer without my sister. I thought it was weird for him to ask me to meet with him without my sister, but I went any way. I wish I

# Ready

had never gone, maybe then I would still have my best friend, my sister. I show up to the address that was texted to me, and it was at Tony Records main office on the 9$^{th}$ floor of this beautiful office building. I was nervous about going in, but I did. I reached the 9$^{th}$ floor, and I exited the elevator, walked towards the receptionist desk and that's when I saw my music producer standing in the waiting room waiting for me to arrive. I walked up to him, and he says, hey Avery I'm glad you came. The receptionist says for us to go right in the office. We walk into this huge room filled with beautiful decorations and Mr. Tony the owner of Tony Records welcomes us in and tells us to have a seat. As soon as we sit down Mr. Tony says he didn't want to waste anymore time and he says that he loved the sound that my sister and I had but he wanted to sign me to his record label. I asked him why only me and he says because my sister was too big, and they just couldn't take a risk of not selling any records, but they promised me that if I did well as a solo artist that we could bring my sister on in a few years and we could present our duet group to the world, but it never happened. I accepted the solo deal because I thought we wouldn't get another chance like this. I was so wrong. We could have

## T & I

made it as a duet group without them I just wasn't confident enough to trust God, trust the gifts God had given us and trust the process. Because of that, I lost the best friend I ever had. I left the office with a $500,000 advance. I went straight to my sister but before I could reach her Tony Records had already put out an official announcement on the radio and on TV that they had signed a new artist called Avery and my sister saw it. She was crushed. When I saw my sister, she told me that she heard the news of me signing the record deal without her and she refused to hear my side of the story and she never wanted to see me again. So, that's what happened between me and my sister. I pray for her all the time, and I even send her letters, but she always returns them to me unopened. I wish I could have the relationship we had together back again but I'm trying to accept reality. Dr. Hicks takes a long drink from her coffee mug and then says, wow Avery, I'm sorry, and I know this is hard, but I have hope that your relationship can be restored. It's going to take some work but if you're committed to trying, we will turn over ever stone and fight to reach out to your sister. Avery says, thank you Dr. Hicks. While you were talking, I wrote out a plan for you to start implementing to start

# Ready

reaching out to your sister, Dr. Hicks says. The first thing on the list is prayer. I want you to start praying that God will allow you an opportunity to be in the same room and most of all, walk in love and forgiveness always no matter the outcome of this situation. I am so proud of you for being brave enough to get your feelings outside of you so that you can grow and evolve. You know forgiveness isn't for the person who hurt you, forgiveness is a personal journey to self-empowerment. Forgiveness only requires you to let go of it and set it free so that God can handle the rest. When you forgive something happens in your atmosphere and it shifts the direction for your future. Happiness and joy are there to fill in that space that unforgiveness occupied for so long. When you have joy, you are more likely to spread joy and love. So, are you ready to forgive yourself, your uncle, the record label, your sister, and the music producer for everything that happened? Avery takes a deep breath and exhales and replies, "yes….. yes I forgive myself for taking the deal and leaving my sister behind, I forgive myself for thinking that I was stupid and that it was my fault that my uncle Elroy hurt me, I forgive myself for damaging the relationship between me and my sister, I forgive my uncle for hurting me for so long, I forgive my music producer for misleading me and aiding in breaking up our singing group for money and I forgive my record label for aiding in the break up of my singing group with my sister. I release it all and I vow to walk in love from this point forward. I am free from it. Dr. Hicks gets up out of her chair, walks over to Avery and gives her a big hug as Avery falls into her arms crying. "I'm proud of you Avery, you did the work and now you're ready for everything God has in store for your future. You're a fighter and you're going to win every time, says Dr. Hicks. You're ready for greatness.

Ready

# Chapter Five

## Ava – Daydreaming

**T & I**

# Ava – Daydreaming

Between the ages of 4 and 6 years old, Ava remembers staring down the long dark hallway of her Uncle Mason's house. Its broad daylight, in the middle of the day as Ava daydreams between clients at the medical office where she works. As Ava zones out she remembers the hallway at her uncle's house being a place of fear, torcher, and trauma. Ava looked so confused and scared because she knew what she just saw in the back room of that house wasn't right for a little girl to see or be a part of. Ava wished she would have stayed outside, but she knew she wasn't supposed to be out there by herself. Ava was full of worry and fear as she tried her best to fight back her tears as she began looking for her sister Avery. Mommy told us to stay together she thought to herself, but Ava knew that something in her just didn't feel right.

Ava called out to Avery as she stood in the living room, but there was no response. Where is she, Ava wondered? Ava frantically ran to the front door to look outside but the little girl saw no one. It was one of those hot sunny days in Georgia and everyone had gone in the house to cool down. Ava turned around slowly and walked back towards the living room, and

## Ready

she stopped at the hallway entry and began staring down the hallway again. All she saw was the sunlight giving light to the back room. Thinking to herself, sissy must be back there somewhere. Ava then built up enough courage to walk back down the hallway. The hallway has dark colored painted walls, and the silence made a simple walk to another room agonizing. While she slowly took each step, she called out for her sister again and again and still no response. She makes it to the doorway of the back room and looks in to see if sissy is in there, but she doesn't see her. Bothered by what she does see, clothes on the floor, bed with no covers, female naked with legs open, and a man walking past her with his pants unbuttoned and zipper down with his private parts visible. Ava says to herself, I'm going back up front. This isn't right and I don't want to get in trouble. Then Ava hears two older girls talking and laughing. The two older girls call Ava's name and tells her to come here. Ava turns around with fear in her eyes and walks back to the room. The older girls told Ava to take her clothes off and get on the coverless bed. Ava looks at them confused because she doesn't know why they would want her to undress. "I'm not dirty. I didn't have an accident in my clothes," Ava said. Then one of the older girls said if you don't do what we tell you, we're going to tell your daddy that you were being bad! Ava was afraid and she didn't want to get in trouble, so she did what they said. As she slowly pulled her pants off, they called their little brother Brayden over. Brayden was around the same age as Ava at the time. The older teenagers told him to take his clothes off too. Ava and her young innocent mind had no idea why the older girls were making them undress. She asked them, have you seen Avery? Where did my sister go? I've got to go find her! All they said was don't worry about Avery, just do what I say do! The little girl wouldn't be able to fathom what these older teens would make her, and their little brother Brayden do next.

Ava lay on the bed and open your legs and Brayden you lay on top of her and rub your body on hers. Now Ava touch him right here and Brayden touch her right there. Pointing and laughing as they continued to force these two kids into adult behavior. The excitement dies down and Ava is able to put her clothes on quickly and runs out of the room and into the kitchen to hide. Ava opens the cabinet door next to the sink and gets in. Ava wanted to scream and cry from the top of her lungs, but she knows

## Ready

that she can't because it would giveaway her hiding place. Hours go by and Ava is still in the kitchen cabinet. As Ava wakes up from her office daydream to her co-worker Amanda snapping her fingers in Ava's face, Ava jumps back in fear losing her balance and falling to the floor and landing on her right side. "What happened", Ava asked her co-workers. Amanda tells Ava that she was walking by the area that Ava was standing in, and she realized that Ava was daydreaming, so she woke her up. Ashley is the office manager at Ava's job, and she is very demanding, and Ava doesn't want to get into any trouble, so she quickly gets up off the floor and gets back to work.

Upon entering one of the patients' rooms with the doctor to observe as a pep smear is being performed, Ava listens to the patient explain what she is dealing with. The patient tells the doctor that she is a recent rape victim and the physicians at the ER suggested that she have a follow-up appointment. Ava hears the word "rape" and immediately drifts off into another daydream. As Ava leans back against the counter, her mind floats back to a time in her childhood when she was at home playing in her room with her sister Avery. Someone knocks on the front door, and they hear voices and laughter break out in the living room. It's their uncle Mason, Braydon, and one of his older sisters. All the adults sat in the living room while Ava, and all the other kids went outside to play. It was a good hot summer day. All the kids were playing and having fun, until Brayon's sister says, "let's play hide and go seek!" Everyone is excited, so they run off to find a good hiding place. Ava quickly runs to the back yard looking for a spot to hide where no one would ever think to look. She quickly climbs the steps to the back of the house and goes in hoping that no one saw her. Ava quietly goes into the laundry room full of clothes and linen, turns around to close the door when she realizes that Braydon and his sister was behind her. Her heart sank in fear as she remembered what happened the last time, they were all alone together. Standing in the laundry room, Ava could hear the other kids talking and running around outside looking for them from the opened window. Ava swiftly says, "I'm going to hide somewhere else, y'all can stay in here!" She tries her best to open the door as fast as she could, but Braydon's sister grabs Ava's arm before she was able walk out.  Her older cousin tells her that she must stay in the laundry room with them, and they could

## Ready

have more fun together alone. Braydon's sister pulls Ava away from the door and stands in front of her to block the door. Ava's eyes began to tear up. She says to herself, "please… not again! I'm at home and this is supposed to be my safe place! Please no! Please no!" She wanted to scream out and call for her mom, but once again her voice was stolen by fear. It was like the fear was a huge scary man with blood shot eyes who had wrapped his hands around her mouth and throat keeping her from making any kind of noise, especially a scream for help! The moment Ava feared was about to come to life. The words she never wanted to hear again burst from her cousin's mouth, "Ava, pulls your pants down! Ava if you don't, I will go in the living room and tell your daddy on you. Feeling like she didn't have a choice, she slowly unbuttoned her pink denim pants and pulled them down as tears began to fall from her eyes to her rosy cheeks. Her cousin turned to her brother Braydon and made him pull his pants down too. Ava was crying uncontrollably and saying to her cousin, "why do we have to do this? I want to go back outside." Braydon started to cry also. He wants to go back outside too. But his sister said no y'all not leaving until I'm done with you both so stop crying! She then

# T & I

told Braydon to rub his private parts on Ava's private area. She asked Ava if she liked it and Ava said no, please tell him to stop. Suddenly, Ava heard her momma calling her. "Ava... Ava... where are you?" The other kids told her that they couldn't find her outside. Then Braydon's sister frantically said "hurry, pull up your pants, and dry you face so you both won't get in trouble." Ava quickly bent down and grabbed her underwear and pants and pulled them up. She buttoned her pants and wiped her face with her shirt. A big sigh of relief came from Ava when she grasped the fact that physically, her moment in hell was over. She couldn't have been happier to hear her mom calling for her.

"AVA... AVA... AVA!!!" Doctor Travis calls her repeatedly. Ava is still standing there leaning on the counter. "AVA ARE YOU OKAY? YOU ARE SWEATING AND YOUR BREATHING IS IRREGULAR!" The patient begins to get very nervous. "Doctor Travis is she okay?" Doctor Travis immediately gets up and calls his other assistances in to help Ava. Ava starts to come back to herself and is very weak and barely able to hold herself up. Doctor Travis instructs his workers to take Ava to an open procedure room next door and she sits down in one of the chairs.

## Ready

Doctor Travis calls 911 and they send an ambulance. Ava's coworker checks her blood pressure and her heart rate. Ava's blood pressure is high, and her heartbeat is still irregular. Doctor Travis comes into the procedure room and says, "the ambulance is here." The EMT's rush into the room and take over. Ava is in tears and is covering her face because she's embarrassed. The EMT's put Ava on the stretcher, strap her in and wheel her out of the doctor's office and loads her into the ambulance as her coworkers, and patient watch on the side lines. The sirens from the ambulance are load and overwhelming for Ava so she starts moving from side to side on the stretcher and saying, "let me out of this thing, let me out now." The EMT tries to calm her down by telling her, "It's going to be okay, we're almost there" but it doesn't help. The ambulance makes a sharp turn into the parking lot and stops. Ava screams, "let me out, let me out, let me out" and then passes out. The ambulance doors swing open and the EMT's rush Ava into the hospital and the doctors take over. Ava's pulse was low, and she was nonresponsive for the first few hours. The doctors and nurses worked hard to stabilize Ava. Once she was stabilized the nurse went out to the lobby to find out who was there with

## T & I

Ava so that she could give them any updates. When the nurse reached the lobby, she yields out, "family of Ava Jones," and Ava's coworkers pop up and quickly ran to the nurse. Dr. Travis says, "I'm Ava's boss." We called Ava's family, but no one is here yet how is she?" The nurse replies I should really speak with a family member, but Ava is stabilized but she seems to have slipped into a comma. That's all that I can tell you right now." Doctor Travis and his staff members look surprised and worried as they make their way back to their seats in the lobby. Doctor Travis tells his staff that he will stay at the hospital until Ava's family comes and for them to go home and get some rest. The staff members leave the hospital. Ava's sister Avery, her Aunt Bertha and her husband **Jonathan** finally make it to the hospital as a loud warning sound goes off in the ER and a rush of nurses and doctors run to one side of the ER to assist a patient. The patient is Ava. Ava's boss walks over to Ava's husband **Jonathan** and says, "he man, I'm so glad you made it. The doctor just told me that she is currently in a comma and that's all I know right now. The doctor wouldn't tell me too much because I'm not family, but they aren't sure what's going on with her, so I've just been sitting here waiting for you to

# Ready

come. I hope and pray that she will make a full recovery." **Jonathan** replies, "thank you so much for getting my wife to the hospital and saving her life." Doctor Travis replies, "no problem, she would have done the same thing for me…. I just want her to get well and come back to us when she's ready. Please keep me in the loop and I'll see you guys later." **Jonathan** replies, "thanks man." Dr. Travis hands Jonathan Ava's personal items, gives him a hug and leaves the hospital.

Aunt Bertha and Avery take a sit in the waiting room and **Jonathan** comes over to join them. Avery says, "what happened? I can't believe I let this go on for this long!" **Jonathan** says, "calm down Avery, just calm down and take a deep breath. Everything is going to be alright." At that moment the ER doctor comes into the lobby and says, "family of Ava Jones." **Jonathan** stands up and walks towards the doctor, Avery runs right behind him to meet him. **Jonathan** says, "hi, I'm Ava's husband and this is her sister Avery, how is she?" With a big smile on his face, he says, "hi, I'm doctor Stanley, I've been taking care of your wife since she came in. The good news is we have Ava stabilized but she is still in a comma, and we aren't sure why she's in a comma. His coworkers told the EMT's that she

## T & I

seems to be daydreaming on the job all day long and just slipped into this comma." Avery begins to cry, and **Jonathan** is overwhelmed with joy. "But we're not out of the woods yet," says Dr. Stanley. Avery blurts out, "Wait, what?!! What do you mean she's not out of the woods yet?" Doctor Stanley simply states, "right now we don't know why Ava slipped into a comma and so we want to run some test. We just want to make sure that we are do everything that we can to find out what this is and prevent this from happening again." Wiping her tears from her face, Avery shakes her head letting the doctor know that she understands. **Jonathan** breaks down as the doctor walks out of the lobby. Aunt Bertha walks over and grabs **Jonathan** and Avery and embraces them both. She says, "everything is going to be okay."

Ready

# Chapter Six

## Ava – Mentally hostage

**T & I**

# Ava – Mentally Hostage

Multiple sounds feel the room as Ava's doctor and several nurses take over Ava's room. Ava flatlined. It was during this time that she had an encounter with God. Somehow Ava found herself suspended in the air above her hospital bed looking down at herself and God was right next to her. Ava says, "am I dead?" God responds no, not yet, you have much to live for." Ava looks down at her lifeless body again and then looks over at the bright light covering God's face and says, "I do? I really don't think so. I'm so broken on the inside; I feel like someone ran me over with a tow truck and just kept backing up and going forward to make sure that I felt the impact. I just don't understand why you'd allow me to be hurt so much as a kid if you care for me so much. I thought you loved me?" God replies, "I created you. Just know that I have a purpose for your life and if I allowed it to happen, I already have a plan. I just need you to let go of it, give it to me so I can do my job." Ava can feel the warmth of God's love, as tears fall down her cheeks like a rushing waterfall, and a feeling of peace feels her heart and mind.

# Ready

As doctors work diligently to revive Ava, she feels a calming come over her because of the presence of God and she doesn't want to leave. Ava turns to God and says, "God I don't want to go back to that world, that world did nothing but hurt me, steal from me, and make me feel like nothing. I can't go back to that. I won't go back to that. It hurts too much. I just want to have peace in my mind like how I was before for anyone touched me. I just want to be normal. Is that too much to ask? This cannot be what life is supposed to be like. I'm living with an instant replay of being raped over and over in my mind. It's almost like I just live there in the rape, like my mind just said let's build our house here and invite all my problems to move in. I was living as if rape was my foundation. It's so bad that now I've started daydreaming on the job. It's like my body just starts a mini movie anywhere it wants, and I just have to go along with the program. I don't want people to think that I'm crazy, so I try to keep it to myself but somehow, I ended up here in the hospital. Now everybody at my job probably thinks I'm the crazy cat lady. What did I do that was so wrong that I deserved to be tormented every day of my

## T & I

life? Why did you let them hurt me? I always get the short end of the stick and it's just not fair. I deserve better, no…. I demand better!" As tears fall from Ava's face, she can feel God covering her whole body from the inside out with His holiness and His love. This is the safest Ava has ever felt in her life. God responses to Ava's rant saying," I love you beyond your ability to process and understand. You are beautifully and wonderfully made with a specific purpose in mind and you were never alone, even in the mist of being hurt I was there, even when you felt like I had left you all alone I was there, even when you said you didn't believe in me anymore I was there and even now, I am here, only this time, it was necessary for me to physically be in your presence so that you could truly feel your fathers love. You are in the right place at the right time. You just need to put every problem, every circumstance, every trial, every person that treated you wrong, every dream, every daydream and even every person in your life that isn't a help to you in my hands so that you can rise up and you can become who I have made you to be, to share your story and to glorify me with your whole heart and mind. You're not going to be perfect, but I will continue to cover you in my love and grace so that

# Ready

you will be protected as you get in position. Ava is in tears on the floor as God says "I release you to return to your body now. Ava slowly gets back up on her feet and tells God, "Thank you, thank you for allowing me to feel what real love feels like. Somehow, I have a sense of new hope to go back into the world and figure out how to shine through all the darkness. I realize now that love is the solution to all the darkness in my life. I love you Lord and I can see it your way now. I'm ready to go back now. The light around God's face becomes overwhelmingly bright as God says, "you got this my child, you will do great things in my name."

Ava wakes up with clarity of mind and a heart filled with love and a willingness to forgive as she scans the room full of doctors and nurses. The doctors and nurses are surprised when Ava wakes up. The doctor decides to run a series test to try to figure out why she was in a comma. As Ava clears her throat to speak, she is in disbelief that she was in a coma. Ava says I feel good, are you sure it was a coma doctor? Ava is still on cloud nine! Her personal encounter with God has her basking in His glory! She feels completely renewed, revived, and rejuvenated. Her encounter with God gave her a perfect view of herself and how she was operating. Now that Ava is aware that her vision was distorted by a plank in her own eye, she knows what the cause of the so-called coma was. She was the cause of her own warped sight. She was purposely holding the plank in her eye keeping it from being removed. As hard as Ava tried to hold her emotions in, she was overjoyed and could no longer hide her facial expressions. As she continued to listen to the doctor's updates and his plan for her care, her smiling face distracts him. I'm sorry ma'am, but I'm totally thrown off by your reaction. Why are you smiling? This is a serious situation! Ava looked at the doctor and said, I do apologize to you and your nurses. What I just experienced you may not understand. I've waited for so long to feel this way again and I can't hold my expressions any longer. Doctor... Doctor please know that I have heard every word you have said to me, and I know you are doing your job and I appreciate all that you and your staff is doing for me. The doctor and nurses are still lost and don't really understand, but they decide to move forward with the testing to find out what caused Ava's coma. One of the nurses walks up to Ava and tells her that her family were all in the waiting room. She says, once the Lab Technician comes in and collects the blood samples and

## Ready

urine needed, your family will be able to come back to see you. Ava thanks the nurses and she turn to walk out the door. The nurse tells her to try to get some rest and to buzz the nurse's station if she needed anything. Ava nodes her head and says, okay, I will. The nurse leaves the room. Sitting up in the bed, Ava lays her back on the pillow and begins to pray a prayer of thanksgiving. Lord I thank you for keeping me and showing me myself! God, I thank you for giving me the tools I need to right my wrongs. Most heavenly Father, I thank you that this was not the end of me. I thank you Jesus for your healing, grace, and your mercy. Master, I thank you restoration! Just before Ava ends her prayer, she falls into a much-needed sleep. While she sleeps, her husband walks in the room quietly and sits the chair beside her bed. As he sits and waits, he closes he eyes to try to calm himself down but his phone rings. It's Aunt Bertha checking in on him and Ava. Hi Jonathan, you ok baby? What did the doctor say about Ava? Is she awake yet? How is she? Jonathan jumps up and quietly runs out the room, trying not to wake Ava. Aunt Bertha… Aunt Bertha! Wait! Hold on! I can't talk much right now. The doctors

## T & I

said she is out of the coma, but she is asleep and resting right now. Aunt Bertha, when she wakes up, I will let you know.

# Chapter Seven

**Ava & Avery – Finding their way**

# T & I

## Ava & Avery – Finding their way

Ava was so grateful to overcome being in a comma and coming out alive. Ava wasn't excited about staying in the hospital to allow the doctors to run more tests, but it was the best choice. It's in the middle of the day and Ava decided to sit up in her bed. Ava's husband was sitting in the chair next to her and when he saw her sitting up, he said, you okay? Do you need something? Ava replies, no, I was just so happy to be here, and now I'm just read to enjoy life. I believe God gave me a second chance at life and I don't want to miss out on it anymore because of the trauma from my past.

Finding your way after a traumatic ordeal happens can be difficult depending on who you have around you, their point of view, and their own person desires for you might not be the right influence. Luckily, Ava's husband is a good man, and he desires for Ava to be the best version of herself.

As Ava sits on her hospital bed looking out the window, she thinks about her sister Avery and wonders if their relationship will ever get better. Ava

## Ready

doesn't know that Avery's been at the hospital for a very long time waiting for her to get better. Ava says to her husband, "baby do you think me, and Avery could possibly rekindle our relationship? Jonathan said to her, "of course. You know Averys been wanting to talk to you for years, but she always felt like you didn't want to talk to her, so she's just been waiting on you. I remember her reaching out to you many times and you shut her down quick. You have been so mean to her and I get it, I know she hurt you but how long are you going to hold that over her head? It's time to let it go and get back to being sisters. So, you think you might want to call her now?" Ava replies "yes, I think I'm ready. I want my sister back. Avery was my best friend, and I haven't had a friend since we broke up and it's been hard. I don't have anyone to tell my secrets to." ………. "Hey…. What about me?" replied Jonathan. "Oh yeah sweetheart, I share things with you all the time but it's different when it's your best girlfriend. I love Avery with all my heart, and I am at a place where I am ready to forgive her. I just wonder will she forgive me for being so stubborn and childish for so long. I just realized that after being in a coma and God blessing me to come out of it still in my right mind is a miracle. I realized just how short and precious life is and I don't want to waste anymore of my time here on earth being upset about the little things. We only get one life, and I don't want to leave this world without knowing that me and my sister's relationship is okay. So, we got to make it right. With a big kool-aid smile on his face, Jonathan passes Ava the phone. Ava dials Avery's number not knowing that Avery was at the hospital the whole time waiting in the lobby. The phone rings and Avery picks up on the first ring. "Ava, I'm so glad you're okay, Avery quickly said. Tears immediately fill Ava's eyes when she hears the joy and excitement in her sister's voice. Ava sighs and takes a moment to gather herself so she could respond. "Will you come see me at the hospital, we have a lot of catching up to do. Avery replied. "Yes, sis I'm already here," and they both hung up the phone. In less than a minute Avery comes walking in the door and they both smile as Avery makes her way to the bed to embrace Ava. Tears begin to fall down their faces as they hold each other tightly. "I am so sorry sis, I was wrong. Will you forgive me?" Avery said. "Yes, I forgive you, but I need to apologize to you as well for being so stubborn, bullheaded, and unreasonable all those times

## Ready

you tried to apologize to me. It was crazy of me to do that and I'm so very sorry sis, said Ava. "No worries sis, all is well now, I forgive you too."

After staying in the hospital for almost a week enduring countless tests and procedures, Ava's doctors enter her room to give her the results of the test. "Hi Ava, I have ran every test that I could think of on you and miraculously I can't find anything wrong with you and since your sister has been here with you, your attitude has changed, your mood is better, and you're always smiling. I don't know what happened, but I do know the power of love. Real love changes things. So, I will be discharging you today. I want you to see your primary care doctor next week for a follow up appointment. Best wishes to you Ava.

As Ava gets up off the hospital bed to get ready to leave, she gets a sudden chill down her back, a feeling of relief. She looks up at her husband Jonathan and says, "babe thank you for being there for me and dealing with me and my crazy moments. Especially when I was being stubborn and stuck in my feelings about Avery." She gives him a big hug. "Babe I really appreciate how hard you fought for Avery and me to reconnect and deal with our problems. You knew I needed my sister back! I see now that I was the main one you had to fight with. Me being difficult almost cost me my life!" Jonathan looks down at Ava with tears in eyes, clearing his throat, he softly tells her, "Ava... Bae I thought I lost you! That really scared me. I didn't know what to do. Words cannot explain, I just can't see myself without you love!" Ava smiles and places her hands on Jonathan's face and wipes his tears away. Jonathan continues to say, "Bae you are the better part of me, that's why I need you here with me. I know how much you love your sister. When I met you, Avery was the first person in your family you told me about, and the first person I had to meet. I had to get Avery's approval for you to even date me girl!" They both burst with laughter as they remembered how it was when they met. Jonathan says sternly, "I know you Bae, and not having that close relationship with your sister broke your heart." Ava closes her eyes and lays her head on Jonathan's chest as he continues to speak, tears flow from her eyes onto his shirt." Ava, you and Avery had a relationship like no other. And when you two opened your mouths to sing together, things happen! God moves! Hearts are filled! When y'all sung, it was like

### Ready

we got to experience the love you had for each other and for music!" As Jonathan held Ava in his arms and kissed her on the cheek, he whispers in her ear, "I'm so proud of you for making that phone call to Avery! Ava you are on the right track. So, whatever you got to do please do it! I won't survive without you Bae."

Jonathan stands up and walks over to the wheelchair in the corner of the room and brings it over to Ava. He stretches out his hand to Ava so that he can help her off the bed and into the wheelchair. Ava smiles so big and extends her hand to Jonathan and slides slowly off the bed into his loving arms. They embrace each other and hold a long romantic kiss and Jonathan says, "everything is going to be alright now. Avery enters the hospital room with a huge smile on her face and says, "ready to go?" Ava looks up at her sister and says, "you bet." As Jonathan begins to push Ava's wheelchair out of the hospital room, Avery grabs Ava's bags and they all leave the hospital with restored hope for their future as a family and the birthing of a duet group that will impact nations.

## T & I

Ava and Jonathan make it back home safely. Ava can't stop smiling as she sits down at the kitchen table. Thinking about Avery, she is overjoyed and excited to see her again. Even though she knows they need to have a serious conversation and lay everything out on the table so they can both heal, it doesn't stop her from smiling. As Jonathan walks towards the kitchen, he catches Ava smiling. Hey Bae! I haven't seen you look this happy in a long time. What's up? Ava says, well I know Avery and I need to have a serious conversation but I'm so happy and thankful that I've got to a point where I can handle it. Ava says with excitement, babe I got my sister back! I'm going to invite her over for brunch tomorrow so we can talk. Jonathan is shocked! Oh, wow Bae! Don't you think you need to take a day or two and rest? You know you just got out the hospital. I hear you babe Ava says to her husband. Babe, I've wasted too much time already and I don't want to wait any longer to get this over with so we can move forward. I know God has specific assignments for us to complete and for a certain group of people to be a part of it. Not only was I holding myself up from what God has for me to do and accomplish, I was stalling everyone else he has assigned to the mission. Ava gets up from the

## Ready

kitchen table, walks in the living room with her phone in her hand and sit on the sofa. As she quickly dials Avery's number, Jonathan sits beside her waiting to eavesdrop on her conversation with Avery. The phone rings once and Avery answers swiftly. Ava are you ok? Did you and my brother make it home safely?! Yes... yes, we made it home and I'm fine. No worries sis, Ava says. Avery, I was just calling to invite you over for brunch tomorrow if you're free. We can talk and get everything out. Avery is beyond excited that her sister invited her over after so long. She is shocked that Ava wants to talk about their issues. As Avery opens her mouth to respond to Ava, she can't help but cry tears of joy. This is something she's waited so long to hear her sister say. Ava asks, Avery, are you okay? Yes Ava, I'm more than okay! I have missed you so much!! Of course, I will be there tomorrow! Avery screams with excitement, "girl I will be there bright and early!" Ava laughs at her sister screaming on the phone. It reminds her the long conversations they had before all the craziness took place. Avery calms down and says, well sis you just got home from the hospital so you go get some rest and I will see you in the morning. Ok Avery, I will chill for the rest of the day Ava replies.

## T & I

They say goodbye and hang up the phone. Ava looks at Jonathan and says, I know you heard all of that Mr. Nosey! Jonathan looks at Ava like he has no idea what she is talking about and gives the biggest smile ever. Babe, I need some things from the grocery store for tomorrow, will you go get them please... Jonathan closes his eyes and lays his head back on the sofa and sighs... yes Bae I will. Ava smiles, kisses him softly and says thanks babe.

It's 9 a.m. the next morning and the alarm clock goes off. Ava rises and turns the alarm clock off. She gets up and makes her way into the bathroom to get dressed. She hurries to the kitchen to start cooking the food for her brunch date with Avery. An hour has passed and the doorbell rings. Ava goes to the door, looks out the little side window to see who it is. It's Avery. Ava opens the door and says well good morning early bird. Avery laughs and walks in the house. Avery states, I was hungry, and I didn't want to wait any longer and plus I knew you were cooking. They laugh and Ava says, girl come on in here and help me finish cooking. Avery follows Ava back into the kitchen. They finish preparing the food

## Ready

and sit down at the kitchen table together. Avery blesses the food, and they began to eat. Silence breaks out in the room because they both knew it was time to start the hard conversation. Avery and Ava didn't want the happy vibe they had from reconnecting to be ruined by this needed conversation. Avery steps up and is first to break the silence. So, Ava, what is it that you wanted to talk about, Avery asks. Ava takes a deep breath in... Well I think we should pray before we dive into that. Avery agrees and they both bow their heads as Ava prays. Dear Lord, thank you for giving me my sister back, now Lord help us heal together and reunite, Amen. Okay sis what I wanted to talk about is how you and I ended up being distant and how our sister-ship was broken. For me I was completely torn apart and broken when you left to do your thing with your music. I thought we both were going to do it together. I felt like you abandoned me. And that triggered some other feelings I had from what happened to me when we were younger. All those feelings just came crashing down on me all at once. The more I saw or heard you out there singing the worse it became. Avery, I admit, I got a little jealous of you too. I really don't know how to handle the hurts of my past, I was victimized and traumatized. So, Avery I am truly sorry for closing the door to my heart to you. I am sorry for not allowing you to explain to me your reasons why you left and did things the way you did. I was wrong. I know it's going to take time and effort from us both to get completely back together, but I'm committed to doing whatever we have to do. I love you and I will never close you out again. Ava, I accept your apology and now I need to explain to you what, where, when, and how. First, I am so sorry that I hurt you. I was so wrong for leaving you and I acknowledge your feelings because you were right to feel that way. There is no excuse for what I did. Our music producer tricked me into coming to a meeting with the label and when I got there I was told that they couldn't take you because of your size but if I were to sign with them they would allow us to do our duet group later but they lied to me. The label put out the news before I could even leave the building and by the time, I had reached you, it was too late but it's my fault and no matter how long it takes I am determined to restore our relationship. Ava wipes her tears away and says, I forgive you sis and I love you and we're going to make it.

## **Ready**

Six months have passed since Ava was discharged from the hospital and was reunited with her sister Avery. Since then, Ava and Avery have faithfully attended counseling sessions separately as well as together. Avery has made it her mission to continue attending church and to restore her relationship with Ava. On top of all of that Ava and Avery started singing together again and the new material that they've created together is nothing short of amazing. When you desire change, change will happen and that's just what Ava and Avery have proven in their life together in the past six month. Avery continues to attend her counseling sessions with Dr. Hicks. She has developed new coping skills to help her deal with challenging situations when they develop. Ava has joined the church choir and her individual counseling sessions have been very beneficial for her. Her confidence is stronger, and she now believes in herself and what she has to offer this world.

Sometimes in life we hit a few bumps in the road and we get us off course and it leads us to an altered way of thinking, and treating others but the good news is, God has the power to reroute us and get us back on track.

**T & I**

We just have to be willing to give the issue to Him so that He can do His job. Are you READY to shift and evolve?

**Ready**

## Acknowledgements

We are so thankful for our ministry partners who have helped us to make this Ready movement happen. We pray that God will continue to bless and keep you as we continue our self-love, and healing journey.

We are thankful for our beautiful parents who raised us to love the Lord and treat others right.

So grateful to God for every person who loves us, sows into us and appreciates us.

We love you all.

**T & I**

Made in the USA
Columbia, SC
24 September 2024